BOB
STAAKE

Bob Staake's

Look!
Another
Book!

L B

LITTLE, BROWN AND COMPANY

New York   Boston

L O

OK!

Another Book!

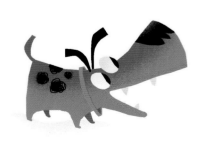 

Once AGAIN

a seek & find,

MORE images

of every kind!

Discover things, both small and large,
you can DO it—just take charge!

Scary monsters, hanging bats,
super-goofy flying cats!
The words are few and far between,
more PICTURES than you've ever seen!

Now open up this crazy book,
grab a seat—and have a LOOK!

Look!

A quack!

A stack!

A checkered yak!

Panic at the SHOPPING MALL! Watch out for that bowling ball!

Look!

An oar!

A tail!

A snail!

A fish reading mail!

RECESS is our favorite time! RUN and JUMP and SWING and CLIMB!

Look to find the lemon-lime!

Look!

● A boot!

● A fruit!

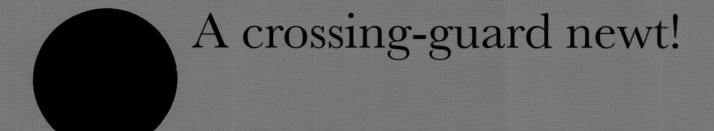 A crossing-guard newt!

 A dog!

A log! ●

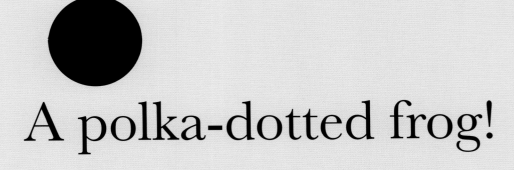

A polka-dotted frog!

UPtown! DOWNtown! High and low! BUSY CITY—go, go, GO!

Search to find the pizza dough!

Look!

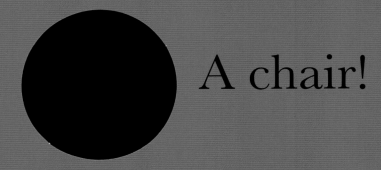 A chair!

A pear!

A miniature bear!

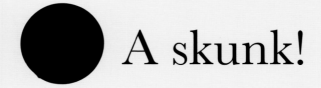 A skunk!

A trunk!

A UFO punk!

All aboard for outer space! Come and play at our MOON BASE!

Can you find the zebra vase?

Look!

Beef stew!

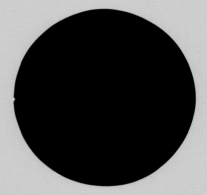 A shoe!

A blue kangaroo!

● A note!

A goat! ●

A teeny red boat!

Watch out when you're at the ZOO—careful, or you'll STEP ON POO!

Quick! Now find the crab fondue!

Look!

A box!

A fox!

A bunch of clocks!

A can!

A fan!

A banana-faced man!

ART MUSEUM (very hip)! Lots to see in one small trip!

Can you spot the red-paint drip?

Look!

A grin!

A twin!

A pink pushpin!

 A spark!

A shark!

Two eyes in the dark!

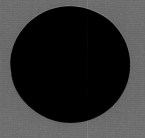

Monster-making SCIENCE LAB—watch out for the ones that grab!

Can you find the taxi cab?

Look!

A rose!

Six toes!

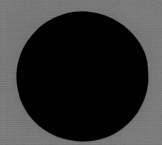

Ice-cream-cone nose!

The End?

Hold on, partner—
whoa, whoa, WHOA!
Chill your saddle, don't you GO!
Yes, you MISSED a thing or two!
(Relax, it happens, buckaroo.)

No, no, *you've NOT* found all the stuff, so NOW this book—it gets MORE tough!

There's
STILL MORE
hidden in
these pages,
so find it ALL.
(It won't take ages!)

(Don't be scared—
just lift it UP!)

C'mon, DO it—
giddyup!

Can you find...

1 panda

2 lions

3 canoes

4 pumpkins

5 teapots

6 big pencils

7 soccer balls

8 ghosts

9 robots

10 slices of cake

11 blueberry bagels

12 green books

Okay!
Okay!

You're REALLY good!
You're SMART.
You FOUND 'em.

(Knew you would!)

Ah yes, you found the giant jack,
you saw the art museum crack!
You spied the gator, found the doughnut,
caught the ad for Super Go-Putt!
You saw the blue goat on the bear,
and found that upside-downside pear!

So MAYBE now this book has taught
that PICTURES—well, they're worth A LOT!

You'll find MORE in this silly book,
so have yourself ANOTHER LOOK!

For Frederick Fleet and Reginald Lee, who looked . . .

. . . a little too late.

—BS

ABOUT THE BOOK

Ever since he was a child, Bob Staake has been known for doing six things at once—and his picture-book process is no different. While writing, rhyming, designing, and illustrating his books, Bob uses a variety of tools to get the job done. He produced the playful imagery throughout *Look! Another Book!* using 2b pencils, Speedball drawing nibs, and extra-black Higgins ink. Then he created the images digitally with Adobe Photoshop 3.0, clicking, squeezing, and tugging a computer mouse which, he says, "feels a little like drawing with a bar of soap." Though Bob didn't actually cut all the holes that appear on each page ("I've never been very good with scissors," he says), he did design a system for seeing through one page to an image on the next.

This book was edited by Liza Baker and designed by
Bob Staake and Patti Ann Harris. The text was set in Baskerville.
The production was supervised by Charlotte Veaney.

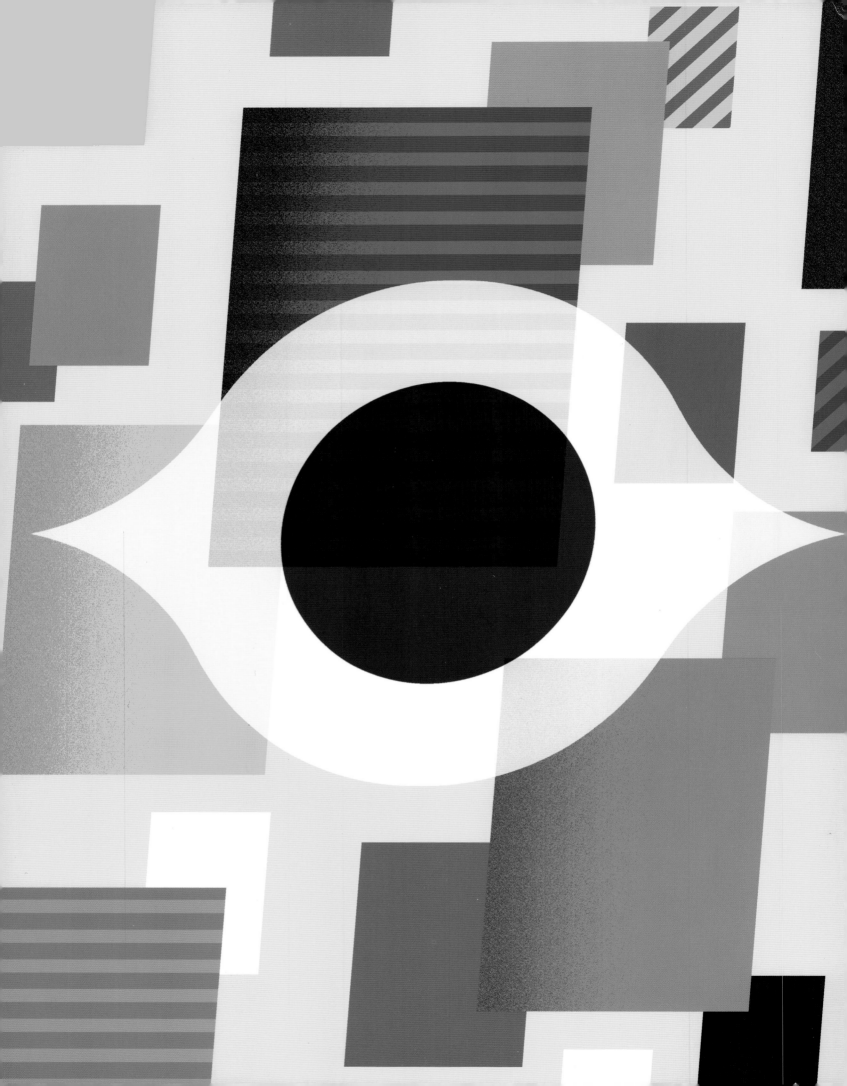